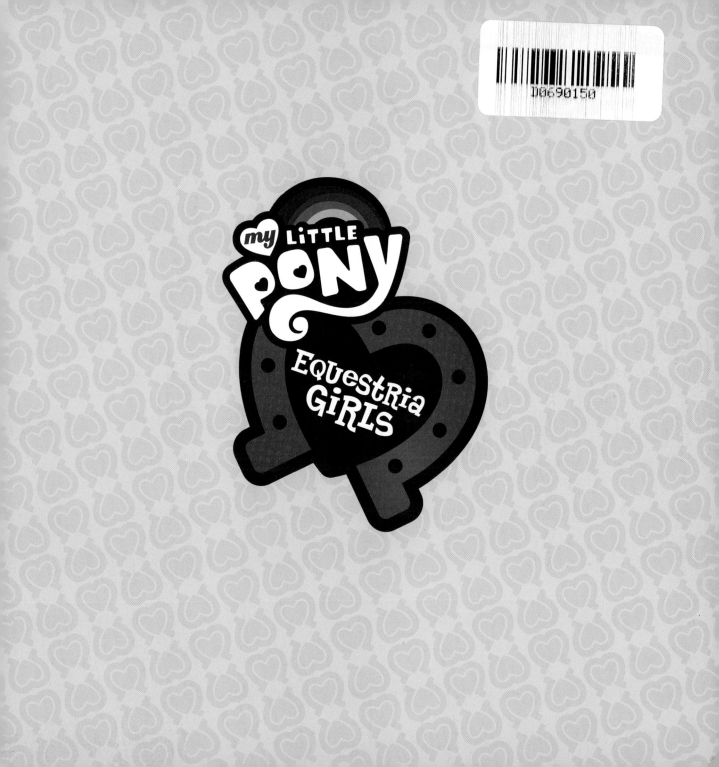

Little, Brown and Company

Hachette Book Group
1290 Avenue of the Americas, New York, NY 10104
Visit us at lb-kids.com

mylittlepony.com

LB kids is an imprint of Little, Brown and Company.
The LB kids name and logo are trademarks of Hachette Book Group, Inc.

The publisher is not responsible for websites (or their content) that are not owned by the publisher.

First Edition: September 2016

ISBN 978-0-316-39530-4

Library of Congress Control Number: 2016944994

10 9 8 7 6 5 4 3 2 1

CW

Printed in the United States of America

Licensed By:

LEGEND OF EVERFREE

SAVE OUR CAMP!

Adapted by Louise Alexander

Based on the screenplay by
Kristine Songco & Joanna Lewis

LITTLE BROWN & COMPANY

LB kids

LITTLE, BROWN AND COMPANY
New York ✳ Boston

On their first night at Camp Everfree, Twilight Sparkle and her friends gathered around a campfire, sang songs, and told stories.

One camper told everyone about the legend of Camp Everfree and how it was named after Gaea Everfree, a powerful magical spirit who once lived in the woods and promised to return...

Some of the campers were scared...but all of them were so excited to be spending a week away from Canterlot High. What sort of fun adventures would they have?

The next day, the campers were already comparing their experiences.

"I love it here," Applejack exclaimed. "We're far enough in the woods to take a break from magic. We can have fun the old-fashioned way: no flying, no tricks...just our own smarts and talents!"

"I don't know. Magic makes it easier and faster to do things," argued Rainbow Dash.

"Yeah, but isn't it nice to enjoy the trees and animals and beauty of the woods?" Fluttershy asked.

As the girls debated the pros and cons of magic, they were interrupted by a perky voice.

"Good morning, Camp Everfree! I'm Gloriosa Daisy, your camp director. It's my job to do anything it takes to make this the best week ever!"

"So, tell me what you want to do!" she said. "Seriously, you can do anything! What will make this the greatest week of your life?"

While everyone chatted excitedly about the endless possibilities, Twilight noticed a limo pull up on the grounds. Its license plate read FILTHYRICH. The very tan man in a very fancy suit who got out looked very suspicious.

Sunset Shimmer leaped in front of Twilight, putting her spying to a halt.

"Come on, Twilight, let's check out the lake! Do you know where the dock is?"

Rainbow Dash rushed up. "I know where to go! This camp is awesome! We can sail boats, go swimming, catch fish...."

As Rainbow rambled on, Twilight smiled. She was so distracted by her friends' excitement for fun that she totally forgot about Filthy Rich.

On the dock, Principal Celestia and her sister, Vice Principal Luna, reminisced about their time at the camp, many moons ago.

"Remember our gift to Everfree?" asked Celestia.

"Oh yes." Luna nodded. "Working together to build something for the camp was one of my favorite activities as a camper!"

As they helped Applejack into a life jacket, a loud crack stopped them in their tracks.

A huge section of the dock splintered apart!

Rarity screamed, "No! That was supposed to be the runway for my fashion show!"

Instead of seeing a crisis, Applejack's eyes lit up. "A new dock, y'all–that should be our gift to the camp!"

While everyone gathered around Applejack to share design ideas, Twilight overheard Gloriosa whisper to herself, "It sure seems like a lot of work. We may not even have a camp next year."

Twilight elbowed Sunset. "You hear that?" Sunset nodded and motioned for Twilight to follow her to their tent.

"Something weird is definitely happening," Sunset whispered. "But it will take an act of magic to fix the dock and help Gloriosa keep the camp open!"

"Oh no, I see where this is going." Twilight shook her head. "You heard Applejack–camp is supposed to be a place where everyone can get away from magic."

"Come on," Sunset begged. "No one will be mad if we use magic to save Camp Everfree!"

Twilight felt torn between taking a time-out from magic and using it to perform good deeds. As she wondered what to do, objects in the tent suddenly lifted off the ground!

"Woah, is that a yes to magic?" Sunset asked in amazement.

"I didn't even mean to do that! See, Sunset, I can't control my own magic! What if using it causes more harm than good?" Just then, the items that had been floating crashed to the ground, making the bunk a disaster zone!

The next day, strange things happened any time Twilight was around.

Pinkie Pie put the *mess* in *mess hall* when a weird cookie-decorating explosion covered the kitchen in batter and sprinkles.

At the rock-climbing wall, Applejack somehow became so strong that she nearly sent Rarity crashing to the ground. Throwing her hands up in frustration, Rarity produced a pulse of light that sent Applejack flying into the lake!

That night, Sunset noticed Twilight sneaking into the woods. She followed her down a path, calling out, "You're worried you're causing all this, aren't you?"

Twilight turned with tears in her eyes. "Magic almost hurt people today! What if I destroy Camp Everfree with my magic? Everyone will hate me and I'll feel terrible! It's like you read my mind, Sunset. I am scared!"

Sunset confessed, "Twilight, all day I've been tuned in to everyone's thoughts and memories, and you know what...I'm starting to think there's something about this place that's bringing out the magic in all of us!"

Just then, a rainbow glow shot out of a cave in the rock quarry. The girls couldn't resist a closer look.

Tiptoeing inside, they found themselves in a magnificent crystal chamber. In the middle of all the sparkling beauty, Gloriosa stood whispering to herself.

"I can't sell Camp Everfree!" she said desperately. "It's been in my family for generations. If Filthy Rich gets his hands on this land...I just know he'll use its magic for evil!"

Sunset saw a flash into the past of Filthy Rich inside Gloriosa's office, laughing. "Face it," he said, "you've run out of money to keep this dump open. I'll see you at the end of the season when you'll be forced to sell it!"

"You can't let Filthy Rich buy the camp, Gloriosa," Sunset pleaded as she snapped back into the present.

Gloriosa turned, shocked to see Sunset and Twilight and even more surprised they could read her thoughts.

"Impossible!" Gloriosa cried. "Plus, I just know you and your friends have had a terrible time here. I don't think the other campers will even care if Everfree closes."

With a far-off look, she declared, "I'm going to have to take this into my own hands."

Gloriosa broke off a handful of the powerful crystals from inside the cave. The crystals suddenly transformed her into Gaea Everfree! "Behold, the power of nature! It's my turn to use magic to keep Everfree safe!" With a wave of her hand, Gaea trapped the girls in a spiral of vines that shot out of the ground.

"NOOOOOO!" As Twilight and Sunset screamed, Gaea floated off, leaving a fortress of branches in her wake.

Back at the yard, campers ran for cover.

Huddling together, Rarity turned to her friends. "We've got to stop Gaea from trapping us in here!"

Applejack nodded in agreement. "This place activated our magic. We have to use it to help Gloriosa come back and save Everfree!"

Fluttershy used her ability to talk to animals to convince some groundhogs to dig escape tunnels for the campers.

Applejack summoned her strength to roll boulders through the wall of branches, while Rarity used the shield to protect her fellow campers. Pinkie Pie decorated it with exploding sprinkles!

Rainbow Dash ran lightning-fast laps around Gaea, creating a tornado of dust to distract her as the friends tried to stop the wall of roots from trapping them forever.

But no matter how hard they tried, they couldn't stop Gaea's wall from growing bigger and thicker.

Just when it seems like the campers would be trapped forever, Twilight and Sunset ran up and joined their friends (thanks to some help from Spike, who chewed them out of the grip of the vines). As they grabbed one another's hands, a white light shot out and Gaea's wall of brambles instantly disintegrated and Gloriosa was back!

In the days that followed, the campers repaired the damage to the camp and, with Glorisa's guidance, set up a fantastic fund-raiser to keep the camp from Filthy Rich! The campers did it! They gave Camp Everfree the best gift.